About the Author

Joan Lowery Nixon is a renowned writer of children's mysteries. She is the author of more than eighty books and a four-time winner of the Edgar Allan Poe Award for the best juvenile mystery of the year. She lives in Houston with her husband.

The Theatre Ghost Mystery

JOAN LOWERY NIXON

Hodder
Children's
Books

a division of Hodder Headline plc

To Katherine Joan McGowan, with love
–J. L. N.

Text copyright © 1995 Joan Lowery Nixon

First published in 1995 by
Disney Press, 114 Fifth Avenue,
New York, New York 10011

First published in Great Britain in 1997
by Hodder Children's Books
a division of Hodder Headline plc
338 Euston Road
London NW1 3BH

10 9 8 7 6 5 4 3 2 1

A Catalogue record for this book is available from the
British Library

ISBN 0 340 68749 5

Typeset by Avon Dataset Ltd, Bidford-on-Avon, Warks
Printed and bound in Great Britain by
Cox & Wyman Ltd, Reading, Berkshire

As Brian and Sean Quinn locked their bikes to the rusty railing outside the old Culbertson Theatre, Sam Miyako, Brian's best friend, rode up and jumped off his bike. He jerked a thumb towards the ambulance and police car that were parked at the curb behind the handful of curious onlookers who had gathered in front of the theatre.

'I came as soon as you called me,' Sam said breathlessly. 'What's going on?'

A paramedic trotted out of the theatre and flung open the ambulance doors. The crowd leaned forward expectantly.

Brian asked Sam, 'Do you remember

1

reading about Clyde Marconi? He's the developer who wants to tear down this block of buildings and build a supermall.'

The Culbertson Theatre was located at the end of a row of old brick buildings that had been boarded up for nearly ten years. The area had been deserted when shoppers and sightseers became drawn to the more modern and convenient malls and restaurants on the other side of Redoaks. A recent editorial in the local Redoaks newspaper had complained that the buildings were an eyesore and demanded that something be done to revitalise the old part of town.

'About fifteen minutes ago,' Brian explained, 'Mr Marconi telephoned Dad. One of Mr Marconi's inspectors was onstage in the Culbertson Theatre when a sandbag fell and hit his shoulder.'

'Your dad told you that?' Sam asked.

Brian smiled. 'Well, not exactly. Dad wrote down the facts of what Mr Marconi said on a pad of paper. The pen he used left an imprint in the soft paper. After he left, I rubbed a pencil over the paper and was able to reproduce the message.'

'Cool,' said Sam. 'But why did Mr Marconi call your dad?'

Sean broke in. 'Last week he hired Dad to investigate some accidents in the theatre.'

'Accidents?' Sam said. 'Like what?'

'A stair railing suddenly broke,' Sean answered, 'and Mr Marconi fell. Later he nearly got squashed by a large stage flat that had been propped against the wall, only he jumped out of the way in time.'

'What's a stage flat?' asked Sam.

'You remember that school play we were in last year?' Brian said. 'Well, a flat's a piece of scenery that's fastened to a wooden frame.'

'Yeah,' said Sean, grinning. 'Like that door that got stuck and wouldn't open when it was supposed to.'

Brian nodded. 'Well, in this case Mr Marconi didn't think the broken rail and the falling flat were unrelated accidents, and he doesn't think the falling sandbag was, either. He's sure that somebody's doing this stuff on purpose, and he's worried about the safety of his crew if he gets approval from the city council to tear down the building.'

Sam narrowed his eyes and made his voice sound scary. 'Mr Marconi is right. They weren't accidents. Everybody knows the theatre's haunted, so you can blame the ghost.'

Sean stiffened. 'Ghost? What ghost?'

'Cut it out, Sam,' Brian said. 'Sean and I are here to help Dad with his investigation. We haven't got time to listen to another one of your ridiculous stories.'

'Yeah,' Sean added. 'We're not little kids anymore, you know. I'm nine now. Anyway, nobody believes in ghosts.' The fact is, Sean *did* believe in ghosts, especially the kinds of ghosts that always appeared in Sam's stories. Sean couldn't help it. The scarier the story, the more he believed it.

Sam grinned. 'It isn't a story. It's true.

The ghost suddenly appears onstage, and he has claws for hands and eyes that burn like fire and . . . Ouch!'

A tiny elderly woman who had been standing nearby rapped Sam sharply on the shoulder with the handle of her umbrella. 'Nonsense,' she declared. 'Horatio was always a gentleman, and his spirit is an inspiring presence.'

The boys all turned and stared at her open-mouthed.

'Horatio?' Sean asked. 'The ghost's name is Horatio?'

'That's correct,' the woman said. 'The ghost of the actor, Horatio Hamilton. Horatio was in very poor health during one of our productions back in 1940. Or was it '41? But he was quite considerate about waiting to die until after the final curtain.

'I am Miss Nora Ann Beezly,' the woman declared. The faded red silk poppies on her straw hat bobbed up and down as she nodded. 'I'm a former actress, director, and occasional playwright.'

Brian, Sean, and Sam introduced themselves to Miss Beezly.

'Hey, look!' said Sean suddenly. The
paramedics were wheeling a man with a
heavily bandaged shoulder out of the
theatre and loading him into the
ambulance.

'Cool!' shouted Sam as he watched the
ambulance speed away with lights
flashing and siren blaring.

Then the bystanders began drifting
away. Miss Beezly sighed. 'I'm sure all
this frightful commotion at the theatre
has quite unnerved poor Horatio.' She
turned to Brian. 'You know, of course,
that some perfectly dreadful man is
planning to tear down the theatre?
Horatio is awfully upset.'

Brian whipped out his notebook and
pen. 'Miss Beezly,' he said, 'are you
saying you actually believe in this
Horatio?'

'Why, of course, dear.'

'You've actually *seen* him?' asked Sean.

Miss Beezly shook her head. 'No. Not

6

seen. But I've felt his presence many times. I regret not visiting the theatre to pay my respects to Horatio. I'll try to find a nice quiet time soon to come by and chat.'

'You probably won't be able to get in,' Brian said. 'They must keep these old buildings locked.'

'Oh, yes. I know they do,' Miss Beezly answered, 'but that doesn't matter. I still have the key I was given years ago when I worked day and night on our wonderful productions.'

Sam said, 'Our drama teacher told us that actors believe all theatres are haunted by ghosts.'

'*Most* theatres,' Miss Beezly corrected. 'By the way,' she said, frowning at Sam. 'Young man, that description you gave of Horatio having claws and burning eyes is utterly ridiculous! The truth is that a ghost who is in residence in a theatre is considered by actors to bring good luck.'

'Why would a ghost bring good luck?' Sean asked.

'It's like having someone on hand to watch over the performers,' she explained, 'to keep them from coming onstage at the wrong cues, or flubbing their lines, or tripping over the scenery.' She shook her head. 'Theatre ghosts certainly don't cause accidents,' she said. 'If you ask me, that terrible man who wants to demolish the theatre is responsible.'

'Mr Marconi?' asked Brian. 'Why do you think that?'

'Yeah,' added Sean. 'He's the one who hired our dad to investigate all the accidents.'

'Accidents, *smack*cidents,' Miss Beezly blurted out. 'I don't trust that Mr Marconi one bit.'

'Why not?' asked Brian.

'He didn't tell the truth when he in-formed the city council and the press that the theatre building is unsound,' she said. 'The Culbertson was built to last forever. Just like me. You tell your father not to trust him, either.

'And would you be so kind as to ask him to please be considerate of Horatio,' she added. 'If he's treated with respect, dear Horatio might even lead your father to whoever is responsible for the accident.'

'How would he do that?' asked Sean.

'Why, through a ghostly message, of course.'

'We'll tell my dad,' Brian said politely.

Miss Beezly smiled. 'I live not far away in the Tinsley Flats,' she said. 'Why don't you boys come to visit sometime? I'll make lemonade and tell you lots of stories about the Culbertson Theatre.'

'About Horatio, too, I hope?' Sean asked.

'Oh, yes. I have many stories about dear Horatio.'

'Cool!' Sam and Sean said together.

Brian wrote down Miss Beezly's address and phone number in his note-book. After the old woman had gone, Brian looked over his notes. Much of what she had said sounded like nonsense, Brian thought, except for the stuff about Mr Marconi and the city council. He would have to check that out later.

'My mum knows Miss Beezly,' Sam said. 'She goes to our church. Mum says she's real nice but kind of dramatic, and she's always forgetting things.' He saw Brian frowning over his notebook. 'I don't know why you bothered to write down all that junk she told us. You don't believe what she said about Horatio?'

'Of course not,' he said. 'But a good investigator checks out everything. Among other things, I want to find out as much as I can about the history of the theatre and its current condition. Miss Beezly could be a valuable resource for that.'

Sam grinned. 'You mean like, is a ghost living in the attic?'

Brian smiled as he tucked his notebook into the pocket of his jeans. 'Why not?' he said. He and Sean had learned from their father that a good investigator doesn't rule out any information without checking it first – even if that means tracking down a ghost.

'Okay,' said Brian finally. 'It's time to meet Horatio.' He began walking towards the theatre door.

'Won't your dad be mad if we show up?' asked Sam as they walked towards the theatre.

'Heck no,' said Sean. 'We've helped him out on a bunch of cases before. He'll be happy to see us.' Then Sean had second thoughts. 'I hope so, anyway.'

'Neat,' whispered Sam. The boys were standing at the top of the main aisle that led down to the stage. It was dark except for thin slivers of light that came through the broken shutters that partially covered the theatre's many windows.

'I bet that a long time ago those windows were used to let in fresh air between performances,' Brian pointed out.

Sean could make out the outlines of the dark stage. It reminded him of a giant yawning mouth. Suddenly he heard low, mumbling voices. Sean moved closer to Brian.

'Brian, I think I heard something.'

'Me, too,' said Brian.

'It's not Horatio, is it?' Sean asked.

'No,' said Brian. 'Not unless Horatio is one of Dad's clients. Look.'

A man walked onstage carrying a torch.

'That's Mr Marconi,' Brian whispered to Sean. Mr Marconi was followed by Mr Quinn and a police officer.

'The city inspector may have classified this building as sound, but I don't think that it is,' Mr Marconi announced.

'We've examined the rope that held the sandbag,' the policewoman said. 'It's old, dirty, and badly frayed. You were right to call us, but there's nothing to indicate that the falling sandbag was anything more than an accident.'

'Well, I disagree,' Mr Marconi said, 'and I've hired Mr Quinn here to investigate.'

There was some more conversation the boys couldn't hear, then the policewoman left, and Mr Marconi and Mr Quinn disappeared backstage.

Suddenly a hand clamped down on Sean's shoulder. 'What are you boys doing in here?' the voice angrily demanded.

Brian, Sean, and Sam whirled to face two well-dressed women, both with scowls on their faces.

'This is not a playground,' the short, plump woman said severely. 'What if you break something? Children are always breaking something. Isn't that right, Dolores?'

The tall one nodded deeply.

Break what? Sean wondered as he tried to wriggle free. The whole theatre already looked pretty broken down to him. Here and there, throughout the sagging rows of seats, clumps of padding spilled through rips in the faded red velvet upholstery.

'We're not here looking to break anything,' Sean began to explain, but the two women would not listen.

'Please leave,' the tall woman said. 'Right now. You don't belong in here.'

'Yes we do,' Brian answered politely. 'Our father is John Quinn, a private investigator, and we're helping him in his investigation of the accidents that are taking place here in the theatre.'

'Accidents?' the short woman said. 'We've only heard of the one accident that took place earlier today.'

'There were two others,' Sean said.

The women looked curiously at each other with raised eyebrows, then nodded knowingly. 'In any case,' the tall woman said finally, 'you're just children. How could you possibly help?'

'The theatre's supposed to be haunted,' Sean blurted out without thinking, 'so we're going to try to find the ghost who might be causing the accidents.'

Brian was about to explain when Mr Marconi, Mr Quinn, and a third man appeared onstage.

'Clyde Marconi!' the short woman shouted. 'Come down here, please! We have something to say to you!'

Sean almost giggled. The woman

reminded him of one of his old teachers at Redoaks Junior School. She was always scolding him in that same tone of voice.

The three men climbed down from the stage and walked up the aisle. When Mr Quinn saw Brian and Sean he frowned, then shook his head. 'Mr Marconi,' he said, 'I'd like you to meet—'

The tall woman angrily interrupted. 'You have undoubtedly forgotten, Mr Marconi, but we were supposed to have had an appointment with you thirty minutes ago. Your secretary told us you were here in the theatre.'

The short woman broke in. 'Although we were previously introduced, Mr Marconi,' she began, 'I'll refresh your memory. I'm Mrs Helen Hemsley, president of the Redoaks Historical Society, and this is Mrs Dolores Rodriguez, our secretary-treasurer.'

'Yes, I remember you,' sighed Mr Marconi wearily.

'Just what are you doing now that is so

important that you could not make our meeting?' demanded Mrs Hemsley.

'Our *scheduled* meeting,' added Mrs Rodriguez with emphasis.

'I'm sorry,' said Mr Marconi. 'I had an emergency.'

'I see,' said Mrs Rodriguez. 'And may I ask what business you and your crew have in this theatre?'

'My inspector and I have been going through all the buildings in this area,' Mr Marconi explained. 'When we tear them down, we want to know what will be involved and how much it's going to cost.'

'Hmmmph!' Mrs Hemsley said. 'You're never going to tear down the Culbertson!'

Mr Quinn stepped in. 'Mrs Hemsley and Mrs Rodriguez, I'd like you to meet Al Duggan, a reporter for the *Redoaks News*. I'm John Quinn, a private investigator who—'

'How do you do, Mr Duggan,' Mrs Hemsley snapped. 'Mr Quinn, there's no need to tell us why Mr Marconi has hired you. We already know. You're here looking for ghosts.'

'I'm . . . I'm what?' Mr Quinn asked in astonishment. He looked at Mr Duggan.

Al Duggan, looking equally surprised, jotted down something in his notebook. 'Ghosts?' he said. 'This is one police call I'm glad I listened to.'

Mrs Rodriguez gave a loud sniff. 'We also know that Mr Marconi is responsible for these alleged accidents in this theatre, not a ghost.'

'Exactly,' concluded Mrs Hemsley. 'He's trying to make it appear that this building is unsound when it isn't. He'll do anything to get his plan approved by the city council. He warned us he was going to get his way.'

'Those were *your* words, as I remember,' responded Mr Marconi. 'You told me I was in for a fight I couldn't win!'

'Oh, come now,' scoffed Mrs Rodriguez. 'Imagine anyone in his right mind wanting to tear down this beautiful old historical building and build a mall!'

'Indeed,' added Mrs Hemsley. 'The fact is you can't claim that the building is structurally unsound because it isn't! So you stage accidents to try to prove that the building is dangerous.'

'Your tricks won't work, Mr Marconi!' thundered Mrs Rodriguez. 'We'll fight you in city council meetings to preserve this building!'

'Now just a minute!' shouted Mr Marconi, who was so angry he looked like a red balloon ready to pop. 'Your accusations are false! I'd never stage an accident! The lives of my employees are at stake!'

Al Duggan broke in. 'Let's get back to what you said about a ghost,' he suggested. 'What did you mean, Mrs Hemsley, about looking for ghosts?'

'The theatre's haunted,' Sean answered without thinking. Everyone turned to stare. 'The ghost's name is Horatio Hamilton. Only Horatio didn't cause the accident.'

'How do you know, kid?' asked Mr Duggan excitedly.

'Miss Nora Ann Beezly said so,' said Sean. 'And my name isn't kid. It's—'

'Sean,' Mr Quinn said, 'I think you've said more than enough already.' He sighed and turned to Mr Duggan. 'I'd like to set matters straight once and for all about this ridiculous idea of ghosts.'

But Mr Marconi ignored him. 'I'm beginning to understand what all this ghost business is about,' he growled. 'You people at the Historical Society dreamed up the idea of a ghost, thinking that a haunted theatre will bring tourists to Redoaks. And you hope that the idea of tourists, with money to spend, will throw the votes of the city council to your side!'

'You're accusing *us* of tawdry theatrics!' shouted an outraged Mrs Hemsley. 'Well, I never!'

'Nor I!' added Mrs Rodriguez. 'Sheer lunacy! Poppycock! You won't get away with it!'

'A beautifully restored haunted theatre

would bring tourists and benefit the entire town of Redoaks,' Mr Duggan suggested to Mr Marconi.

'Here! Here!' chimed Mrs Hemsley and Mrs Rodriguez.

'If you want to benefit the town,' Mr Marconi countered, 'then stop these tiresome old busybodies from getting in my way, and let me build my mall! Think what the town would gain in additional taxes!'

'Old busybodies!' the two women fumed.

Mrs Hemsley, Mrs Rodriguez, and Mr Marconi began arguing louder and louder. It was like a contest to determine who could outshout the other.

Sam nudged Brian. 'Check out the reporter. He actually seems like he's enjoying this.'

Mr Duggan was taking notes as fast as he could, and he had a huge grin on his face.

It wasn't the reporter Brian was worried about. His father looked very angry, and it didn't take a genius detective to figure out why. Brian and Sean had helped their father on cases many times, but Brian knew his father would be unhappy that they hadn't talked to him first before showing up at the theatre. It didn't help, either, that they had been responsible for spreading the story about the ghost.

'It's kind of noisy in here, Dad,' Brian said. 'We'll see you at home.' He murmured to Sean and Sam, 'Come on. We'd better get out of here . . . fast!'

SUPER 3 SLEUTHS

Mr Quinn didn't arrive home until seven that evening, just in time for dinner. It appeared to Brian that his father was now in a better mood. He just hoped they could get through dinner without anyone mentioning ghosts.

'John,' said Mrs Quinn as she dished up plates of spaghetti, 'what's all this about a ghost in the Culbertson Theatre? A story in this evening's *Redoaks News* reported that a string of mysterious accidents had occurred there. It also said that the theatre is haunted and even quoted Nora Ann Beezly. Is it true you think a ghost is responsible for the accidents?'

Brian groaned and sneaked a look at Sean, who was too busy cramming pasta into his mouth to notice.

Mr Quinn sighed. 'It's just a ridiculous story from a reporter more interested in headlines than the truth.'

Mrs Quinn smiled. 'For many years Nora Ann Beezly starred in plays at the Culbertson. When I was a little girl I thought she was so glamorous! My goodness, she must be well over eighty years old now.'

'Miss Beezly was nice,' Sean said. 'We met her in front of the theatre. She told us the ghost is named Horatio Hamilton, and she even invited us to come and see her sometime.' Sean took another bite of spaghetti and mumbled through it. 'And Miss Beezly said Horatio didn't cause the accidents because he's a polite, kind ghost.'

'Sean,' Mr Quinn said, putting down his fork and looking at his son. 'We don't talk with our mouths full, and we don't believe in ghosts. There is absolutely no logical explanation for ghosts.'

Mr Quinn went on to discuss people who thought they saw things because they allowed their imaginations to get out of hand, but Sean stopped listening and began wondering what it would be like to meet Horatio Hamilton. Miss Beezly had said Horatio was polite and kind, he remembered, but wouldn't the ghost look scary anyway?

'By the way, Dad,' Sean said, 'Miss Beezly asked us to tell you to be considerate of Horatio.'

Mr Quinn gave a long, patient sigh. 'Were you listening to one single word I said?' he asked Sean.

One single word? thought Sean. 'Sure, Dad,' he answered. He knew he'd even listened to more than just one word. 'I was only giving you a message, that's all.'

'There's more to the message, Dad,' Brian said. 'Miss Beezly doesn't trust Mr Marconi.'

'Did she say why she doesn't trust him?'

'She doesn't want him to tear down the

theatre,' Brian answered. 'She seems to think he misled the city council in his report on the conditions of the building.'

'Miss Beezly does have a point,' Mrs Quinn said. 'The theatre's a beautiful building. It was built back at the turn of the century, when the style was to add lots and lots of elaborate decoration. I can still remember the cupids and roses that were painted on the ceiling.'

'According to what Mr Marconi told me, it would cost a fortune to restore the theatre,' Mr Quinn said. 'For one thing, the building would have to be completely rewired and all the seats replaced. New carpeting, new lighting fixtures . . . You can see how expenses would add up.'

'On the other hand,' said Brian, 'the new mall would mean more taxes paid into the city treasury. The city council would like that.'

'The newspaper article claims that the Historical Society plans to come up with most of the restoration money,' Mrs Quinn said. 'They know it's going to take time, but once they get approval from the city council they can start raising the money.'

'Dad,' Brian said, 'those women from the Historical Society said a city inspector classified the building as sound, but Mr Marconi says it's dangerous. Are you going to find out who's right?'

'My job is to find out for Mr Marconi if the accidents really were accidents and if they weren't, then who's to blame.'

'Did you complete your investigation of the theatre?'

'Yes. I looked through every inch of the backstage area this morning,' Mr Quinn said. 'I couldn't find anything out of the ordinary, and the theatre equipment seems to be safe enough.'

'Is that what you told the police?' asked Brian.

'Yes,' said Mr Quinn. 'They were more than satisfied with my report.'

'Then are you going to do a computer search, the way you usually do?' Brian asked.

'I've already begun,' his father said.

'How can you find a gho— I mean, anything about the accidents on a computer?' Sean asked.

'The computer gives me important background information about the individuals involved in the case – even my own client,' Mr Quinn said. 'For example, I can find out if Mr Marconi has ever been involved in lawsuits and if he and his backers have acceptable credit ratings. And I can do the same check on the members of the Redoaks Historical Society.'

'But Dad,' Brian persisted, 'what if someone really did push the flat on Mr Marconi, or take the screws out of the railing, or even cut and pulled an old piece of rope so it looked like it was frayed? Isn't all that possible?'

'Yes,' his father said, 'it's possible. But what would the motive be?'

Sean looked at Brian, who smiled. He knew that his older brother had already begun figuring out an answer to exactly that question.

SUPER
4
SLEUTHS

'When we begin *our* investigation of the
theatre it won't do any good to take
fingerprints,' Brian said as he rummaged
through his private investigator's kit.

'Right.' Sean was flopped across Brian's
bed. 'Ghosts don't leave fingerprints.'

Brian laughed. 'Forget about Miss
Beezly's so-called ghost,' he said. 'I'm
talking about *human* fingerprints. Mr
Marconi and his inspector, the police,
and the paramedics have all been in the
theatre. Their fingerprints will be all over
everything.'

Next to his notebook and pen, Brian
placed two torches, a magnifying glass,

three small plastic sandwich bags, and a pair of tweezers. 'All set,' Brian said.

Sean pointed at the bags and tweezers. 'Do you really think you're going to find some kind of evidence?'

'I don't know,' Brian said. 'Remember, Dad told us that a criminal always takes something away and, in turn, leaves something behind. It could be an oil stain or grass from his shoes or . . .'

'Ghosts don't wear shoes.'

'The kind of ghost we're hunting for might.'

'I don't get it,' Sean said. 'Are we going to try to find Horatio or not?'

'Let's just say that we need to take a good close look at the theatre,' Brian told him. 'Can you meet me there after school tomorrow?'

'Just you and me?'

'And Sam and Miss Beezly,' Brian said. 'I'm going to call her and ask if she'll come with us. Remember, she has a key.'

*

30

The next day Sean couldn't stop thinking about Horatio.

Who cared that Brian didn't believe in ghosts! Sean thought. The idea of maybe meeting a real ghost was so exciting that Sean couldn't keep it to himself. At noon, in the Redoaks Junior School cafeteria, he told his friends Matt and Jabez what he and Brian were going to do. 'Want to come?' he asked.

'No way,' Matt said. He dumped some ketchup on his gooey macaroni cheese and stirred it up. 'I read about that ghost in the newspaper. If he's causing accidents, then I don't want him coming after me!'

'Me, neither,' Jabez said with a grin. 'Ghosts are sickening, with their bones hanging out and their arms and legs dropping off.'

Sean laughed. 'Where'd you ever see a ghost like that?'

'Everywhere,' Jabez said. 'The movies ... MTV.'

Debbie Jean Parker plopped onto the

bench beside Sean. 'Don't be dumb,' she said in a superior tone. 'Real ghosts kind of shimmer around, and you can see through them. Everybody knows that. I'll go.'

'Huh? You'll go where?' Sean asked.

'With you,' Debbie Jean answered. 'You asked who wanted to go. Well, I've always hoped to see a real ghost, so I'll meet you at the theatre.'

Matt rolled his eyes at Jabez. 'Debbie Jean and Sean are going on a date.'

Everyone said that Debbie Jean Parker was Sean's girlfriend. The truth was, Sean thought she was just about the grossest girl on the planet. In the universe!

As Jabez hooted, Sean scowled at Debbie Jean. 'You weren't invited,' he said.

'You invited Matt and Jabez.'

'That's different.'

'The only thing that's different is they're too scared to go, ha-ha, and I'm not.'

'Take her with you, Sean,' Jabez told

him. 'If the ghost drops chunks of decaying flesh all over the floor, make Debbie Jean pick them up.'

'Yeah,' joked Matt. 'There are rules against littering in a theatre!'

Matt and Jabez whooped with laughter.

With a sniff of disgust, Debbie Jean stood up and glared at Sean. 'I'll see you there,' she said, and walked away.

That afternoon Sean concentrated so hard on his maths test that he forgot all about Debbie Jean. He didn't remember her until he rode his bike to the theatre and saw that she'd managed to get there before he did.

Miss Beezly, whose hat was trimmed with purple roses, turned from Debbie Jean to smile at Sean. 'I'm so glad you invited this dear little girl to join us,' she said.

Dear little girl? thought Sean. Yuck! As Miss Beezly beamed at Debbie Jean, Sean crossed his eyes and pretended to stick a finger down his throat.

Brian and Sam rode up. They chained their bikes to the railing, next to Sean's bike, and greeted Miss Beezly.

As Miss Beezly unlocked one of the main doors to the theatre, Debbie Jean clapped her hands together and gave a squeal of delight. 'I hope the ghost shows up. I've always wanted to see a ghost!' she said.

Sam took her arm and pulled her aside as the others entered the building. 'You don't know what the ghost is like,' he said in a creepy tone of voice. 'He has claws for hands and eyes that burn right through you.'

'Oh yeah?' Debbie Jean said. 'Well, don't forget the decaying arms and legs dropping off, and the chains rattling, and the moans and groans.' She pushed past Sam and entered the theatre.

Sean and Sam had brought torches so they could explore backstage, and Brian had brought an extra one for Nora Ann Beezly.

'I'll just borrow this for a while,' Debbie

Jean said, and took Sean's torch.

She led the procession down the aisle, shining the beam of her torch on the stage. 'What a great place to put on our class play!' she said, and turned to Miss Beezly. 'Did I tell you that I'm an actress, too? I had a major part in our last class play.'

'It was *Old MacDonald Had a Farm*, and Debbie Jean played the pig,' Sean said.

'Quiet!' Brian held a finger to his lips. 'I thought I heard something.'

'Was it metal, and did it clink and rattle?' Sam whispered.

'Sam, be quiet!' said Brian.

Everyone stood without moving, listening intently. Finally, Brian said, 'I guess it was just my imagination.'

Miss Beezly spoke firmly. 'Brian is right about being quiet,' she said. 'Horatio is not going to appear if you're making un-necessary noise, and I think it would be a good idea to contact dear Horatio and discover what he can tell us about the cause of the accidents.'

'Wow!' Debbie Jean said.

'Uh, Miss Beezly,' Sean suggested. 'Why don't we explore the backstage area instead?' He had been excited by the idea of meeting a real ghost, but now that it might actually happen he wasn't so sure it *was* a good idea.

'We can do that, too,' Miss Beezly said.

She pointed towards the nearest row of seats. 'Suppose we all sit down and close our eyes and try to become receptive?'

Sean wasn't at all convinced that he wanted to become receptive – as Miss Beezly had put it – but Miss Beezly sat down and closed her eyes.

Brian shrugged and sat down. So did Sam and Debbie Jean.

I might as well get it over with, sighed Sean as he sat down, too. He closed his eyes and hoped for the best.

For a few minutes there was only silence. Then, in a stage voice that carried throughout the theatre, Miss Beezly called, 'Horatiooo? Horatio

Hamilton? It's Nora Ann. Are you here, my dear?'

Sean clung to his seat. He could feel his palms beginning to sweat.

'Horatio, we're waiting,' Miss Beezly called.

If Horatio did choose to answer, Sean knew he'd set a speed record racing out of the theatre.

The wait grew longer and longer. 'I'm afraid it's no use,' Miss Beezly said finally. 'Apparently, Horatio is not willing to join us.'

Sean secretly sighed with relief, but Debbie Jean jumped to her feet, crawled over the seat in front of her, and scrambled across the orchestra pit and climbed up the stairs to the stage.

She stood at centre stage in front of the broken footlights and held her torch up like a microphone. 'This is a great place to perform,' she said. 'Listen to how the sound carries.'

'The Culbertson was noted for its perfect acoustics,' Miss Beezly said.

'I'm going to sing,' Debbie Jean said. She proceeded to wail out a popular country tune: 'My Phone Is as Dead as My Love Life.'

Sean clamped his hands over his ears. 'If you don't stop, we're going to puke!' he yelled.

Then something strange began to happen. As Debbie Jean continued to sing, an odd, scraping sound came from somewhere at the rear of the stage and a peculiar greenish light began to glow upward behind her. It was a hideous, grimacing, glowing head! And as the head rose from the floor, a body dressed in tattered, shimmering robes rose with it – Horatio's ghost!

'My phone is broke, and my heart is, too!' Debbie Jean was singing so loudly that she was unaware of the ghost that towered behind her. The ghost raised one claw-like hand – in which it held a large, gleaming knife.

Sean tried to shout a warning, but he was so scared his voice didn't work. He tried to jump up, but his legs didn't work, either. It was as if they were frozen.

Suddenly Debbie Jean stopped singing. 'Hey!' she said. 'What's wrong with you guys? Don't you even know a great singer when you hear one? I—' She turned and for the first time saw the ghost that was looming over her. Debbie Jean let out a bloodcurdling scream and bolted from the stage.

Terrified, Brian and Sam grabbed Miss Beezly's arm and whisked her up the aisle and out of the theatre. Sean ran right behind them.

Brian slammed the theatre door closed, and Miss Beezly handed him her key so he could lock it.

'My stars!' she exclaimed as she fanned herself with one hand. 'That certainly wasn't Horatio!'

'That was so cool!' said Sam.

'Cool indeed,' said Miss Beezly as she straightened her hat. 'And most exciting.'

Brian, Sean, and Sam gratefully accepted Miss Beezly's offer of cookies and lemonade and walked with her to her flat. As they piled their jackets on a chair and crowded onto the sofa in her tiny living room, she said, 'I'm so sorry the ghost frightened your dear little friend.'

Sean chuckled. Now that he was away from the theatre, his encounter with the ghost didn't seem nearly so frightening. 'I never saw anybody run so fast!' he said.

'She won't be back to bother us.' He held up his glass of lemonade like a microphone and imitated Debbie Jean. 'You huuung up the phone like you huuung up my hearrrt!'

'Now, now,' Miss Beezly said. 'Never be unkind to a performer who is trying her best. Debbie Jean's voice may need training, but you must admit it has clarity and power.' She took a sip of lemonade and smiled. 'Mmmm, lovely,' she said. 'This time I remembered to put in the sugar.'

'It's very good lemonade,' Sean said politely. He put his glass down and reached for a cookie.

Abruptly changing the subject, Brian said, 'I'd like to know what caused that apparition. And why it appeared.'

'Maybe we can find out by talking to Tyrone Peabody,' said Miss Beezly.

'Who's Tyrone Peabody?' Brian asked.

'A very old friend,' Miss Beezly answered. 'Tyrone starred opposite me in three – or was it four? – plays. No one loves the Culbertson Theatre more than he does. Why, he's even appointed himself the unofficial caretaker of the building.'

'The theatre doesn't look like anybody's taken care of it for a long time,' Sean said.

'What does Mr Peabody do to take care of the theatre?' Brian asked.

'He's replaced a few broken windows and patched a small hole or two. Fortunately, the roof is sound and hasn't leaked.' Miss Beezly smiled, and for a moment her thoughts seemed far away. 'Tyrone has made sure that everything in the theatre remains just as the actors left it.' She smiled. 'There are still costumes in the wardrobe, make-up in the dressing rooms, and even some cans of paint once used on stage sets.' She sighed. 'The Culbertson was like home to Tyrone. He still stops by almost every day to relive happy memories. I don't know what he would do if that theatre were ever torn down.'

'He wasn't there today,' Sean said.

'I told him we were going to visit the theatre, but he said he had other plans and couldn't join us.'

'When can we meet Mr Peabody?' Brian asked. 'I hope he can answer some questions for us.'

'And give you a backstage tour,' Miss Beezly suggested, clapping together her hands. 'Are you free tomorrow afternoon? Would you like to return to the theatre then and meet Tyrone? I know he's always free on Tuesdays. That's the day we play bridge together at the senior citizens' centre.'

'Thank you, Miss Beezly,' Brian said. 'Going through the theatre with Mr Peabody would be a good idea.'

'W-w-what?' Sean sputtered. 'You want to go back in there with that horrible g-g-ghost? Why don't we just let Dad solve this case?'

'Yeah,' said Sam. 'The ghost made it pretty clear that he doesn't want us inside the theatre.'

'That's why we can't give up our investigation,' Brian told them. 'There's a logical explanation for the accidents. There's also an explanation for whoever – or whatever – was chasing us out. We just have to find the answers.'

'Good for you,' Miss Beezly said. 'I'll see you tomorrow afternoon, as soon as school is over.'

After they left Miss Beezly's flat, Brian said, 'The county courthouse isn't far from here. Let's go. I want to find out who owns the property around the theatre.'

Inside the courthouse, the boys made their way to the records department, where a clerk was seated behind a desk.

'How do we find out the names of property owners?' Brian asked.

'Do you have lot numbers or property addresses?' asked the clerk.

'Uh, no,' Brian said. 'It's the old part of town around the Culbertson Theatre.'

'I'll give you plats of that area.'

'Plats?' asked Sam.

'Plats are maps that give the recording numbers of each lot,' the clerk explained. 'You can use those numbers to look up the property owners.'

With the clerk's help, the boys located the plat they were looking for.

'Look,' said Brian, pointing at a section of the map. 'Except for those two lots, Mr Marconi owns most of the area west of the theatre.'

'That area had nothing but old rented houses on it,' Sam said. 'What would he want with those?'

'Maybe nothing,' Brian answered. 'He'll probably evict the tenants, tear down the houses, and build something else on the land.'

'You mean like flats or office buildings?' Sean asked.

Brian nodded. 'With a complex under construction, the value of that property would go way up.'

'Who owns the other two lots?' Sam asked.

Brian jotted down the lot numbers,

looked them up, and whistled. 'Robert Hemsley.'

'Hey!' Sean shouted. 'Wasn't Hemsley the name of one of those women from the Historical Society?'

'Right!' said Brian. 'Let's find out who owns the Culbertson Theatre.' He studied the plat, then shook his head. 'It's held in trust by a bank. I don't know what that means. I'll ask Dad about it later.'

The clerk who had assisted them earlier returned. 'Is there anything else I can help you with?'

'No, thanks,' Brian said.

The clerk gathered up the material and returned it. Brian, Sean, and Sam left the courthouse. On the steps outside they came face-to-face with Al Duggan.

'Well, well,' Al said. 'What brings you boys to the courthouse? Looking for ghosts?' He smiled. Brian thought he sounded condescending. Brian was used to adults acting like that. They rarely took anything a kid did seriously.

'Just doing some research,' Brian answered.

'For your father?' Al asked, suddenly interested. 'Want to tell me what you found?'

'Sorry,' Brian said, 'that's confidential information.' He ran down the rest of the steps, with Sean and Sam right behind him.

That evening at dinner Mr Quinn asked, 'Did you boys have a good day?'

Sean nodded. 'We had a big maths exam, and I think I'll get an A, and I even managed to eat the cafeteria food without dropping dead.'

'Where were you after school?' Mrs Quinn asked.

Sean grinned at Brian. 'Watching Debbie Jean practise her hundred-metre dash. She could make the Olympic team.'

'Well, well,' Mrs Quinn said. 'I didn't know Debbie Jean was interested in athletics.'

Sean snickered into his glass of milk,

getting some of the milk up his nose, until he caught his father's frown.

'Dad,' Brian said, 'we found out something interesting today,' and he told his father what they had discovered at the courthouse. Brian asked his father about the bank owning the Culbertson.

'Actually,' explained Mr Quinn, 'Mr Marconi and a group of wealthy investors are trying to purchase the Culbertson. Until the city council votes on whether he can tear it down, the bank is holding it in trust.'

'Sounds complicated,' said Sean.

Mr Quinn smiled. 'It is. By the way,' he said, 'when you were at the courthouse, did you check the tax rolls, too?'

'No,' Brian said.

'If you had, you would have found that Robert Hemsley owns quite a bit of property in the outlying area around the Culbertson, under a corporation name.'

'Is Robert Hemsley related to the woman from the Historical Society?' asked Sean.

'They're married,' said Mr Quinn. 'Why?'

'Just curious,' said Brian. 'Dad, I understand how Mr Marconi could profit if he develops the area, but if the mall isn't built, how could that help the Hemsleys?'

'I'm not sure exactly,' said Mr Quinn. 'But it's a good question.'

Sean spoke up. 'Remember last summer when we were on holiday and Mum wanted to see those historic houses? And there was a restaurant and gift shops and antique shops and a motel? Maybe that's what the Hemsleys have in mind.'

'You mean restoring the theatre so they can make money from the tourists who come to visit?' suggested Brian.

'And don't forget that by having the city council vote to preserve the theatre, the value of the property around it would skyrocket,' said Mr Quinn. 'And because it would be a historic landmark they would get special tax breaks from the city.'

'But I don't understand what all that has to do with the theatre and the gho—'

'Sean!' Brian said sharply. He realised the last thing his father wanted to hear was more talk about ghosts haunting the theatre. Sean saw his brother's look and nodded.

'What were you going to say about the theatre?' Mr Quinn asked.

Sean said the first thing that came into his head. 'Uh . . . about the sandbag that fell,' Sean said. 'I don't get it. Why was a sandbag hanging on a rope in the first place?'

'A theatre has a variety of curtains,' Mr Quinn told him. 'The old Culbertson has a painted asbestos curtain that used to hang just behind the footlights. It was raised before each play began. Behind that curtain is a red velour curtain called the act curtain, which closes off the stage. It was opened for each act and closed between acts.

'Behind the act curtain are black curtains that hang to the stage floor.

They're called legs and are used to hide the wings of the stage where the actors enter and leave. Then there are the black curtains, called borders, that hang above the stage, and drops that—'

'Dad!' Sean interrupted, trying to escape one of his father's long explanations. 'You haven't said anything about the sandbags.'

'I was about to,' Mr Quinn said. 'In the older theatres the curtains were raised and lowered on pulleys, and sandbags were used for weights.'

'So backstage there'd be lots of ropes?'

'That's right.'

'Is it hard to cut through a rope?'

'Not if you have a sharp knife.'

Sean dropped his fork. *The ghost had a knife!*

Sean looked at Brian, but Brian gave a slight shake of his head.

Brian was right to warn him, Sean knew. Now was not the time to tell Dad that a horrible glowing monster-ghost had risen right out of the stage floor.

They'd have to find out more about what
they had seen before they told Dad
anything about it.

SUPER
6
SLEUTHS

The next morning, when he arrived at school, Sean met Debbie Jean. He grinned and said, 'I never saw anybody run as fast as you did yesterday.'

'Yeah?' she said. 'Well, don't forget you were running right behind me!'

'You should have stuck around. We got cookies and lemonade.'

'Oh, sure,' she scoffed. 'From the ghost, I suppose.'

'No, from Miss Beezly,' Sean said. 'She invited us to her apartment, and she told us about Tyrone Peabody, who's a caretaker at the theatre. He's going to meet us there after school today.'

Debbie Jean gasped. 'Are you kidding?' she said. 'You're going back to the theatre? Even after that awful ghost thing came after us yesterday?'

'It may not have been a real ghost, just somebody pretending to be a ghost. Investigators have to check out everything, including ghosts,' Sean bragged. 'Anyhow, I don't think he was coming after all of us. He was headed towards *you*. Your singing probably drove him crazy.'

Debbie Jean frowned as she thought. 'That might not have been a ghost? Well, if you're going to the theatre, then I am, too,' she said.

Sean gave up and grumbled, 'If you insist on coming, then bring back my torch.'

'I will. And I'll bring my dad's superspotlight, too. Whoever that was – ghost or not – we have to get rid of it. Someday I may want to star in a play at the Culbertson Theatre!'

Sean imagined Debbie Jean acting on

the Culbertson stage. People would be glad to pay *not* to come. 'If you do, I'll be in charge of the box office,' he offered, and almost doubled over laughing.

'You're weird,' Debbie Jean said.

'Thanks.'

That afternoon, when Brian and Sam arrived at the theatre, they joined Sean, Debbie Jean, and Miss Beezly. They were talking to a tall, thin white-haired man whose unhappy expression made it obvious that he didn't like them being there.

Unconcerned, Miss Beezly smiled at Brian and Sam from under a straw hat swathed in clouds of pink veiling and introduced them to 'my dear Tyrone Peabody'.

'I think we've met before, Mr Peabody,' Brian said, 'but I don't remember where.'

Mr Peabody looked startled. 'I'm sure we haven't,' he said. 'You're too young to have seen me onstage.'

'Miss Beezly tells me you're the

caretaker for the theatre,' Brian said. 'By any chance were you in the theatre when the sandbag fell and hit Mr Marconi's inspector?'

'No, I wasn't,' Mr Peabody said. 'If I'd been on hand, I would have hurried to help him. I know first aid.' He turned his attention to the others in the group. 'Against my better judgement I accepted Miss Beezly's invitation to give you a backstage tour, so let's get started.'

'I remembered to bring my camera,' Sean whispered to Brian. 'Who knows? I may get a picture of the ghost.'

'Come, come, let's start the tour,' said Mr Peabody as he led them into the lobby.

Inside the theatre Miss Beezly sank into one of the aisle seats in the back row. 'I know the backstage of the Culbertson as well as I know my own name,' she said, 'so there's no point in my taking the tour.'

Brian felt uneasy about leaving her alone. 'I think we should all stick together,' he told her, 'in case that – uh – *thing* comes back.'

'If it does,' Miss Beezly said in a theatrical voice, 'instead of running I shall confront it and find out who it is and what it wants!' Her face crinkled into a smile, and she patted Brian on the hand. 'Now run along and enjoy the tour. I'm sure you have a little ghost hunting in mind.'

'We are not here to go ghost hunting!' Mr Peabody scowled down his long nose. 'Over all these years, I have never seen a single ghost in the Culbertson Theatre – not even the ghost of Horatio Hamilton.'

'So you say,' sighed Miss Beezly as she wiggled into a comfortable position. 'Off you go!' she said, shooing them on their way.

Brian would have felt better if they had all stayed together, but there was nothing he could do about changing Miss Beezly's mind, so he followed Mr Peabody.

'To begin with,' Mr Peabody explained as he walked down the aisle, 'the ornamental arch that separates the stage from the auditorium is called a proscenium arch.'

'Is it true that you've never even seen Horatio?' Sean asked.

Mr Peabody stopped. 'Do you want a backstage tour,' he barked impatiently, 'or do you want to talk about ghosts?'

'Both,' Brian said. 'We want to understand more about the theatre because we want to help our dad solve the mystery of who – or what – has caused the accidents to Mr Marconi and his inspector. We'd like to hear whatever you can tell us.'

'Even though you don't believe in ghosts,' Sean added.

'As for the inspector,' Mr Peabody said, 'he should have known better than to walk under hanging equipment.'

'Where did the sandbag fall?' Brian asked.

Mr Peabody pointed. 'There,' he said, 'right centre. If he had been standing just a foot closer...' He gave a shudder. 'As for the existence of ghosts,' he said, 'I didn't say that I didn't *believe* in ghosts. I said I hadn't *seen* them.' Lowering his voice, he leaned forward and murmured, 'Lately I have noted a few. . . odd occurrences that might cause some people to think that ghosts may indeed haunt the Culbertson.'

'Oh yeah?' said Sean, his eyes widening. Mr Peabody nodded gravely.

'For example,' he said, 'certain objects in the dressing rooms have been moved. Since the building is locked, there was no one here to move them. Just this afternoon I found the wardrobe door hanging open in one of the dressing rooms.'

Sean shivered. 'Do you think Horatio was responsible?' he asked.

Mr Peabody shrugged. 'It's hard to say.'

Brian was less interested in ghosts than in discovering more about the theatre. 'The women from the Historical Society said a city inspector classified the building as structurally sound,' he said. 'Would you agree?'

'Hmmmph!' Mr Peabody snorted. 'Given half a chance those dreadful women would bring decorators in here to change the character of the theatre completely.' Mr Peabody sighed. 'On the other hand, if the theatre is torn down, it will be even more of a tragedy. The Culbertson is a magnificent old building. It should be left in peace exactly as it is.'

Mr Peabody took a deep breath to steady himself. 'Okay. Let's get a move on,' he said. He snapped on a torch and puffed his way up the stairs to the stage. The kids flicked on their torches, too, and followed him.

'Watch your step,' he called back. 'And whatever you do, don't touch anything, especially the ropes.'

'Jeez,' Debbie Jean whispered to Sean, 'what a grumpy old sourpuss.'

A forest of ropes ascended into the darkness. Mr Peabody insisted that the kids stand back as he pointed out the tattered remains of the different kinds of curtains and showed them the pipes with lighting instruments hung on them.

'These things are called battens,' he explained, 'and they're pulled up and let down by the stagehands who are in charge of moving the scenery.'

Sean made sure the flash was in the On position on his camera and began snapping pictures. He took pictures of the ropes, the curtains, the sandbags, and the battens. He even accidentally photographed Debbie Jean posing as a famous movie star.

'Guess who I am?' she cooed.

'Quasimodo?' said Sean.

'The battens look heavy,' Brian said, changing the subject.

'They are,' Mr Peabody told him. 'Now come along and I'll show you the stars' dressing rooms, which are just behind the stage.'

Sean wanted a closer shot of the battens, so he stepped over some equipment and steadied himself by grasping one of the ropes. As Sean aimed his camera, Mr Peabody turned, and a look of terror suddenly came over his face. 'Look out!' he yelled. The battens above Sean's head began to waver.

'Sean!' shouted Brian.

He grabbed Sean's arm and jerked him to one side of the stage just as one end of the battens snapped and slammed to the floor.

Sean stared, his heart banging so loudly it hurt his ears. 'It crashed right where I was standing!'

'I told you to stand back!' cried Mr Peabody. 'I told you not to touch the ropes!' Brian noticed at once that Mr Peabody was as frightened as Sean.

'I was just taking pictures,' Sean said.

'Where you shouldn't have been!'

'The battens didn't fall by themselves,' Brian said.

Mr Peabody walked out to centre stage and looked up before he answered. 'They might have. The ropes are old, and the equipment is probably unstable.'

'I'd like to look at that rope,' Brian said.

'No! Stay back! It may not be safe,' Mr

Peabody warned, but Brian had already taken the end of the rope in his hand and stepped far enough back so that he was no longer under the hanging equipment.

'It's frayed,' he said as he studied the feathered ends of the rope.

'I told you all this equipment is old,' Mr Peabody said.

Brian dropped the rope and wiped his hands on his trousers. The rope had been awfully dirty and dusty.

'It could have been the ghost,' Debbie Jean whispered. She turned to stare at the spot on the stage where the greenish glowing ghost had appeared during their last visit.

Sean stared, too, holding his breath. 'Brian,' he said.

But Brian was pointing at the empty seat in the back row of the theatre. Where was Miss Beezly?

Brian and Sean ran down the aisle, with the others following. But they froze in their tracks when they heard the same strange creaking sound that had accompanied the appearance of the ghost the day before.

They turned slowly towards the stage. The severed head of Miss Beezly, in its frothy pink hat, was resting on the stage floor. The eyes in its head looked directly at Sean.

'It's exactly as I suspected,' said the head matter-of-factly.

'She can still talk!' Sean yelled.

Debbie Jean screamed at the top of her lungs.

'You have a powerful set of lungs, dear, which is a distinct advantage for an actress,' Miss Beezly said. 'But please don't scream again. It hurts my ears.'

Slowly the head of Miss Beezly rose up from the stage floor. In a few seconds Miss Beezly's arms and legs and shoes became visible, too. She stepped forward. 'I don't know why I didn't think of it before,' she said as if scolding herself.

'Think of what?' Sean managed to ask.

'I followed a little side corridor that led to the basement, and sure enough there was a ladder right under the trapdoor. It's obvious that our so-called ghost had no one with him to work the levers that raise the platform, so he used a ladder.'

'A trapdoor!' Brian exclaimed. He rushed back onto the stage.

'Oh, yes,' Miss Beezly said. 'The trap is very cleverly hidden from the audience in the orchestra level, and even onstage you'd need much better lighting than this in order to see it clearly.'

She giggled. 'Do you remember, Tyrone dear, when we produced *Blithe Spirit* and my lovely flowing white dress got caught in the trapdoor?'

'I remember only the excellence of your performance, Nora Ann.' Mr Peabody gave a stiff little bow.

Leaving the two of them to talk about old times, Brian, Sean, Sam, and Debbie Jean rushed to look at the open trapdoor and the short folding ladder that stood open beneath it.

'Shine your spotlight down there,' Sean told Debbie Jean. 'I want to take a picture.'

'Look at all the footprints in the dust!' Brian said. 'There are a lot of big ones Miss Beezly didn't make. And ghosts don't leave footprints!'

'That's weird,' Sam said, and pointed. 'Do you see those places where the ladder's glowing?'

Brian climbed down a few rungs to take a closer look. 'It's green phosphorescent paint,' he said.

'I bet it's the same stuff that was on

whoever was pretending to be a ghost,'
Sean said.

'You mean the ghost isn't real?' groaned
Debbie Jean. Sean thought she sounded
disappointed.

'*That* ghost may not have been real.
But don't forget,' said Sam, slipping into
his scary voice, 'Horatio's supposed to be
hanging around here somewhere.'

'Don't do that!' Sean snapped nervously.

'What's the matter, Sean?' asked Debbie
Jean. 'Are you scared?'

'No,' said Sean defensively. 'And
anyway, I'm not the one who practically
set a world record running away!'

'Oh yeah?' said Debbie Jean.

'Yeah!' said Sean.

'Cut it out, both of you,' Brian said as
he climbed up the ladder of the trapdoor
onto the stage. 'We're dealing with
somebody who's pretending to be a
ghost, and we don't know why.'

'So what do we do now?' asked Sam.

'We look for a motive,' Sean said, and
Brian nodded. Sean knew how Brian's

mind worked when they were investigating a case.

'You've got a motive,' Sam said. 'I could see those women from the Historical Society being really interested in the idea of a ghost that would lure tourists to the theatre after it's restored.'

'But why would the ghost want to scare *us* away?' Sean asked. 'We're not working for Mr Marconi.'

'But we *are* working to help Dad on this case,' Brian said. He stared at Sean. 'And some of us might believe in ghosts and spread the word that the theatre is haunted. You saw how interested that reporter was about Horatio.'

'Yeah,' Sean agreed. 'Since that article came out I bet most of Redoaks believes the Culbertson is haunted.'

Brian pulled out his notebook and turned back a few pages. 'Let's go over some of what we already know.' He began reading. 'A heavy flat almost hit Mr Marconi. A stair railing broke, and he fell. Then on Saturday a sandbag landed on his inspector's shoulder.'

'And don't forget that today the battens nearly clobbered me!' Sean said.

'And don't forget that both Mr Marconi and Mrs Hemsley have big investments in the land around the Culbertson,' Debbie Jean added.

'What's really strange,' Brian said, 'is that the ghost didn't appear to Mr Marconi or the inspector. We were the first – and only – ones to see it.'

'Aha!' Sam said, jabbing a finger into the air. 'That sounds like a clue.'

'The *answer* might be an important clue,' said Brian as he tucked his notebook into his pocket. 'But before we can know for sure we'll need to see more of this theatre, like the dressing rooms and all the backstage places where someone could hide and put on costumes and paint. It might make it easier to learn who our ghost is.'

'Yeah,' Sam said. 'Mr Peabody said somebody had disturbed the theatre stuff.'

'Are we going back there now?' Sean asked.

'Sure. Now,' Brian told him.

Sean turned to Debbie Jean. 'I'll trade you my torch for your superspotlight.'

'No way,' Debbie Jean said.

Brian walked towards the backstage area, but Mr Peabody suddenly called out, 'Wait, young man! Where do you think you're going?'

'We want to inspect the rest of the backstage area, Mr Peabody.'

Sean was amazed at how fast Mr Peabody hopped up the stairs to the stage. 'No, no! We can't have that!' he said.

'You said you'd take us on a tour,' said Brian. 'We haven't seen the dressing rooms yet or the basement or—'

'And you won't,' Mr Peabody said firmly. 'In spite of what happened to the land developer and his employee, I hadn't fully realised the dangers of this old theatre. As I just told Miss Beezly, I made a dreadful mistake in allowing you to be here.'

'We'll be careful! We promise!' Brian said quickly.

But Mr Peabody shook his head. 'No. We're leaving right now,' he said. He shooed them up the aisle and out of the theatre.

With a dramatic flourish, he locked the doors and pocketed his key.

'Thank you, dear,' Miss Beezly said as she waved farewell to Tyrone Peabody. 'Now then,' she said brightly, 'how would you like a cup of cocoa? With marshmallows?' She included everyone in her smile.

Sean was ready to accept. He loved cocoa and marshmallows.

But Brian declined. 'No thanks, Miss Beezly,' he said. 'We've all got homework to do.'

'Huh?' muttered Sean.

'C'mon, Sean,' said Brian. Sean noticed that Brian had a strange look on his face.

'Thanks for everything, Miss Beezly,' said Brian.

'What's the matter with you, Brian?'

Sean complained when they reached the end of the road. 'We don't have that much homework.'

'I know,' he said, 'but we've got to make plans for our next visit to the theatre.'

'You heard Mr Peabody,' Debbie Jean told him. 'He said he won't let us inside the theatre again.'

'We don't need Mr Peabody to let us in,' Brian said. He reached into the righthand pocket of his jacket and pulled out a key. 'Miss Beezly and I both forgot that she gave me her key to lock the door the last time we were there. I still have it!'

SUPER 8 SLEUTHS

Later that evening Brian and Sean
studied the photographs Sean had
brought home from the one-hour camera
shop.

'They're too dark,' Brian finally said.
'They don't show enough detail.' He
tossed the photos onto his bed. 'I wonder
if somebody could have lowered that
rope and frayed it with a knife before we
got there.'

Sean was surprised. 'But then they'd
have to make the frayed rope ends look
old. Could they do that?'

'Maybe,' Brian said. 'There was a lot of
dirt and dust on the rope. I suppose it

could have been rubbed into the ends.'

'Do you think Mr Marconi did it?' Sean
asked.

'I don't know,' Brian said. 'Mr Peabody
kept warning us to get back. What if he
had frayed the rope and knew the
battens might fall?'

'You don't think he would have tried to
hurt me?' Sean asked.

'I noticed he was just as frightened as
you were,' Brian said.

'But he kept telling us to stand back,'
countered Sean. 'It's not his fault that I
walked under the battens.'

'He may have wanted the battens to
fall,' Brian explained, 'but not on one of
us. When you walked out under the
battens it surprised him.'

'Brian,' Sean gasped suddenly. 'Mr
Peabody yelled out a warning to me
before the battens fell.'

'Right,' said Brian nodding.

'He has a motive,' Brian said. 'He told
us he's against the plan to tear down the
theatre.'

Sean nodded. 'And he said he thought that the Historical Society would ruin the Culbertson.'

'That's right! He wants to make sure the theatre stays just the way it is. And he's an actor. Who better than an actor to pretend he's a ghost?'

'Are you sure?' asked Sean.

Brian shook his head. 'No.' He stared at Sean for a few moments. 'We've got to make plans for tomorrow,' he said.

'What about tomorrow?'

'When we go back to the theatre.'

Sean didn't like that idea at all. 'I don't think we should use Miss Beezly's key without telling her.'

'It's okay. She didn't tell us to stay out of the theatre.'

'But Peabody did.'

'He hasn't any real authority. Only the bank that holds the theatre in trust has authority. Think about it,' Brian said eagerly. 'Somewhere in the theatre is the evidence we'll need to prove who is behind all this.'

'But Brian,' said Sean, 'Dad already made a thorough investigation.'

'Dad might have missed something. That's why we have to try. But,' Brian said, 'if you're too scared to go with Sam and me tomorrow morning. . .'

'I'm not too scared!' Sean shouted. He stopped abruptly. 'How can we go tomorrow morning? We have to go to school.'

'The schools are closed. It's an in-service day for teachers. So there's nothing to keep you from searching the theatre. Are you coming with us?'

'I'm coming,' Sean agreed reluctantly. He even managed a smile. 'At least this time we won't have Debbie Jean butting in. Right?'

Brian and Sean woke up before seven, gobbled down cereal and toast, and met Sam, who was already on his bike, waiting for them in the drive.

They cycled to the theatre and chained their bikes to the rusty railing. As they walked quickly to the door of the theatre, they carefully looked up and down the street. No pedestrians were in sight, and traffic was light, with no one seeming to pay attention to them.

'Go for it!' Sam whispered.

Brian unlocked the door, and they slipped into the lobby.

In a hushed tone Brian again went over the plan he had made. 'We start with the dressing rooms, and we stick together at all times,' he said.

'Exactly what are we looking for?' Sam asked.

'Anything that's out of the ordinary, that doesn't seem to belong in the theatre,' Brian explained.

'*We* don't belong in the theatre,' Sean reminded him.

'Besides us,' Brian said. 'We want to find something that can lead us to the person who is haunting the theatre. Come on. Let's go. And keep it quiet!'

'Why do we have to be quiet?' Sean asked Brian. 'We're the only ones here, aren't we?' But Brian didn't answer. 'Well? Aren't we?' Sean asked again.

Sam chuckled. 'Don't forget about Horatio!'

As silently as possible the boys entered the theatre, walked down the aisle, and climbed onto the stage.

Sean tugged at Brian's arm and pointed at the spot where the outlines of the trapdoor were barely visible. 'Somebody closed it,' he whispered.

'Mr Peabody probably came back later,' Brian answered.

'More likely it was Horatio.' Sam grinned.

Brian held a finger to his lips and motioned the others to follow. He turned on his torch and made his way back-stage, past the ropes and pulleys and the fallen battens.

Off to the left were two rooms with their doors open. A mirror inside one of them reflected the beam from Brian's torch, so he walked to the doorway and directed the beam around the room. Sam leaned over his shoulder and examined the room, too.

The mirror was ringed with lightbulbs, and an empty make-up tray rested on the table under it. An old sofa and chair were on the other side of the room, and a painted folding screen leaned against the wall. 'This is probably the way an actor's dressing room ought to look,' whispered Brian.

Sean stepped to the open doorway of the other room. It appeared pretty much the same except for a large jar of white face powder that was overturned on the dressing table. That's funny, Sean thought. The powder looked as if it had been recently spilled. Then he noticed a paint can in one corner. Paint in a dressing room? Sean gave a shudder. Mr Peabody had said he'd occasionally found things out of place. Horatio, he thought nervously.

'Hey, look,' Sean said, but Brian and Sam had gone into the other dressing room. Sean could see the beams from their torches. 'I'm not going to stay out here by myself!' he said, and ran to join the others.

He found Brian and Sam examining the inside of the closet and the drawers in the dressing table.

'Hey!' Sean said. 'This dressing room is neat compared with the other one.'

Brian closed the bottom drawer. 'I thought Mr Peabody said he kept *every-thing* neat. What was in the other one?'

'A messy paint can and a box of spilled white face powder on the dressing table. Come on. I'll show you,' Sean said.

He stood by the open door as Brian and Sam entered.

'What paint can?' Brian asked.

'What face powder?' Sam asked.

Sean bounded into the room. 'Right there!' he said. He stared, his mouth open. The paint can and the jar of face powder – even the spilled powder – were gone!

SUPER
9
SLEUTHS

Brian quickly checked the inside of the
small closet, then carefully shone his
light around the room. He walked back
to the sofa, lifted the flounce that
touched the floor, and pulled out a shoe
that was protruding.

'Whoever was here left a shoe,' he said.
The shoe looked new.

'Just one shoe?' Sam looked at the shoe
and laughed. 'That's not Cinderella's.'

Brian reached under the sofa and pulled
out a matching shoe. 'I'll bet this shoe
matches the prints we found in the dust.'

'You mean whoever owns these shoes
is our ghost?' asked Sam.

'That's right,' Brian said. 'And most likely he's the one who staged the accidents, too.'

'Whoever it was left in a hurry,' Sam said.

'Let's tell Dad and let him take care of it,' Sean suggested.

'No time for that,' Brian said. 'Whoever it is is probably still in the theatre.'

'He is!' Sean stepped backwards nervously, then turned towards the doorway. He stopped and screamed, 'It's him! It's the ghost! '

The ghost stood in the dim corridor outside the dressing room. It was tall and glowed with an eerie green light. It slowly raised its hands. Sean noticed that its fingers were bent like claws. It took a few steps towards him and growled.

'Leave this place! Leave before it is too late!'

Sean gulped. 'H-h-how about a t-t-trade?' he said in a trembling voice. His knees shook like castanets. 'G-g-get out of our way and let us go and w-w-we'll give you back your shoes.'

The ghost slowly lowered its arms. 'I warned you,' it said in a hollow, menacing voice. 'You should have stayed away from here. You do not belong here!'

'You're not a ghost, and you can't scare us,' Brian said. 'We have more right to be here than you do. We're helping our father investigate a case.'

'No one has more right to be here than I do!' answered the ghost.

Sean was shaking so hard he thought he might bounce out of his shoes. He couldn't believe how calm Brian was acting. Then he saw something in the ghost that seemed familiar. 'Brian!' he whispered suddenly. 'What are you doing? You're making the ghost really mad.'

'I know who the *ghost* is,' Brian said, and nodded. 'It's Mr Peabody.'

The ghost let its shoulders slump. Then it shrugged. 'How did you know?'

'You were standing outside the theatre the day the paramedics were called,'

Brian explained. 'And you were listening when Sam talked about ghosts in the theatre, weren't you?'

Mr Peabody nodded.

'My guess is that you staged the accidents in order to discredit Mr Marconi. You knew that the Historical Society would be suspicious, and they were.'

'How would that help?' asked Sean.

'Mr Peabody knew that both groups had motives to be suspicious of each other. And as long as they kept fighting one another, the Culbertson would stay just as it is.'

'But what about the ghost?' asked Sean.

'He decided to use a ghost to scare us away,' Brian said. 'That's why we were the first to see it.

'You also insisted that you hadn't been at the theatre when the inspector was hurt,' Brian said. 'But later you pointed out exactly where he'd been standing when the accident occurred. You gave yourself away.'

'I love the Culbertson,' Mr Peabody

cried, 'and I want everyone to stay away from it and leave it alone. I couldn't allow this marvellous theatre to lose all its beautiful old dignity at the hands of those women who want to restore and redecorate it. And I certainly couldn't stand by and watch it being torn down.' He snuffled. 'Nobody was supposed to get hurt.'

'But the inspector was hurt, and the battens could have fallen on Sean.'

'That's not my fault! I'd warned all of you to stay back and not touch the ropes!' Mr Peabody groaned and wrung his hands. 'Now what shall I do?' he murmured. 'Until I decide, I supposed I'd better lock you in here where no one will hear you.'

A voice from near the stage suddenly screeched, 'Sean! Brian! Where are you guys? Why'd you come without me?'

As Mr Peabody whirled towards the sound, Brian and Sam ran past him into the corridor.

As Sean ran out, Mr Peabody made a

grab for him. Sean slid just under his reach and continued running.

Brian, Sean, and Sam dashed through the backstage area and onto the stage, where they crashed into Debbie Jean Parker.

'Hey, what's up?' she asked. 'You guys look like you've just seen a ghost.'

Debbie Jean, of course, claimed all the credit.

'I saved your lives,' she said smugly. 'If I hadn't shown up at just the right time, there is no telling what might have happened to you. If you want to send me flowers or sweets, skip the flowers. I like chocolates.'

Fat chance, Sean thought. He wasn't going to use his allowance to buy Debbie Jean chocolates.

Immediately after their escape Brian telephoned his dad and explained what had happened. The police arrived a short time later at the theatre. They found Mr Peabody sitting alone in the dark in one of the dressing rooms, mumbling to himself about 'old times'. Mr Marconi, Mrs Hemsley, and Mrs Rodriguez, who'd been meeting in Mr Marconi's office, also arrived, as did Mr Quinn and Al Duggan, the reporter.

Even though Mr Marconi and the women from the Historical Society could no longer blame each other for the ghost and the accidents, they resumed their argument.

Al Duggan took notes while the police questioned Brian, Sean, and Sam. Then he had questions of his own: 'When did you realise the apparition wasn't a real ghost? Have any of you boys ever seen a ghost? Have you seen or talked to the ghost named Horatio?'

Sam decided to play a joke on the reporter. 'Ah, I have countless stories about zee ghosts,' he droned in his fake scary voice. 'I will be glad to tell you . . .'

Brian pulled Sam away from Mr Duggan. 'This was my dad's investigation,' he said, refusing any more questions. 'We just happened to catch Mr Peabody in his act. I don't think we should turn what happened here into a ghost story.'

'But the ghost angle is a good one,' countered Mr Duggan. 'Our readers will love it.'

'Thanks, but no thanks,' said Brian firmly. Mr Duggan shrugged. Just then Mr Quinn walked up.

'Since the police have finished questioning you,' he said, 'there's no need for you to stay here.'

'Dad, what is going to happen to Mr Peabody?' Brian asked. 'In spite of everything he did, I feel kind of sorry for him.'

'Yeah,' Sean said. 'I do, too.'

'Mr Peabody will get the care he needs,' Mr Quinn answered. 'Now, as I was saying . . .'

The argument between Mr Marconi and the ladies was getting louder.

'Dad,' Brian said, 'we found out who caused the accidents, but nothing's really helped that much. Listen to Mr Marconi and those women from the Historical Society. They're still arguing. Mr Marconi wants the mall, and the members of the Historical Society want to restore the theatre. They're never going to get together.'

'Then why don't they do both?' Sean asked. 'They could build the mall around the theatre.

Brian stared at Sean in surprise. Then he said, 'Sure. Why not? After the theatre is fixed up, the Historical Society could put on plays and have tours, and people would come to the mall just to visit the theatre.'

Debbie Jean clapped her hands. 'And I could produce, direct, and star in our class play at the Culbertson!'

Sean had his mouth open to tell Debbie Jean what he thought of that idea when his father clapped him on the shoulder.

'I think you've come up with an ideal solution,' he said. 'I'll propose it to the group.'

As Mr Quinn ushered Mr Marconi and the Historical Society members out of the theatre, Miss Beezly hurried in, the yellow pansies on her hat bouncing as she walked.

'Oh dear, dear!' she cried. 'I was on my way here when I saw and heard the police car go by, so I hurried right down. A policeman told me about Tyrone. Oh dear!'

'Don't worry about Mr Peabody,' Sean said kindly. 'Dad said he'll get the care he needs.'

Miss Beezly sighed. 'It's not just Tyrone I'm concerned about. This entire episode must have been very unpleasant for Horatio.'

Suddenly a breeze blew down the aisle, ruffling the pansies in Miss Beezly's hat and whisking back Debbie Jean's hair.

'Noooora Annnnnn,' a hollow voice murmured.

'Oh, there you are, dear Horatio,' Miss Beezly whispered.

Al Duggan gulped, then stared at Miss

Beezly. His mouth was hanging open.

'You wanted a ghost story,' Brian called out to him as they began to hurry out of the theatre. 'Now you've got a ghost to interview.'

'That was neat,' Brian said to Sam and Sean outside. 'I wonder how Miss Beezly did that trick with her voice.'

'Who says Miss Beezly did it?' Sam said, and they burst out laughing.

'Hey,' said Sean, looking around. 'Where's Debbie Jean?'

'She ran out ahead of us,' Sam said.

Sean smiled. He didn't think Debbie Jean had a chance as an actress. But as the next Flo Jo? As fast as she ran, no one could touch her!